Happy to meet you!

Who are you ?

I'm Luna Rona!

Who are you?

Hi, I'm Rue!

What are you  ?

I'm a type of germ called a virus!
I am the virus COVID19 - my
friends call me Luna Rona!

What do you like to do, Luna Rona?

I like to play with lots of friends so I can spread!

How do you find friends?

Lots of ways! I hang out with people everywhere they go.

I like to play with their
eyes, mouth, and nose.

That's how I spread so fast to
those that are exposed.

What happens when you play with your friends, Luna Rona?

I like playing with my friends.

It helps me grow, but then
really quick my friends sometimes get sick.

That's not nice,
Luna Rona!

Why do you make your
friends sick?

I don't want to be mean.

I have to do what I do because I can't make my own energy. I have to grow to survive. I just spread to stay alive!

How can we play together and stop you from making too many friends sick?

Your number one task is to wear a mask!

Always wash your hands for
20 seconds.

If you're sick,
        stay home in bed.

Stay 10 steps away so that
I don't spread.

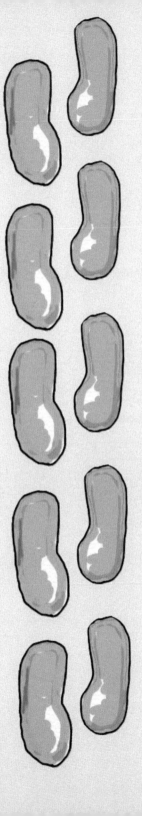

Luna Rona, how will I feel
if I get sick?

You might feel hot, have a cough, runny nose, upset tummy or feel crummy.

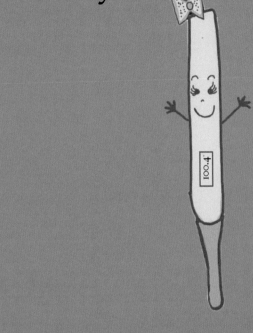

Your parents will take you to get a test, when the swab tickles your nose, don't be distressed!

Then what do I do?

Do not worry

Adults will help you recover until
you feel your best!

Drink water, take medicine, and rest.

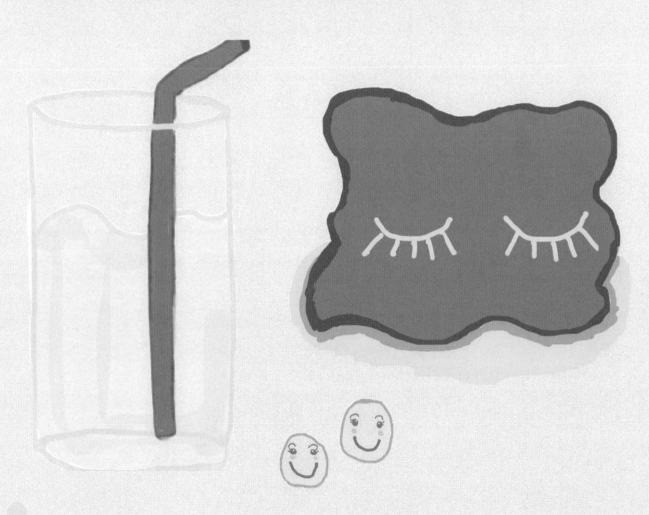

When I feel better, does that mean you're gone forever?

Viruses like me come and go.

After we play, I leave you with a gift called immunity!

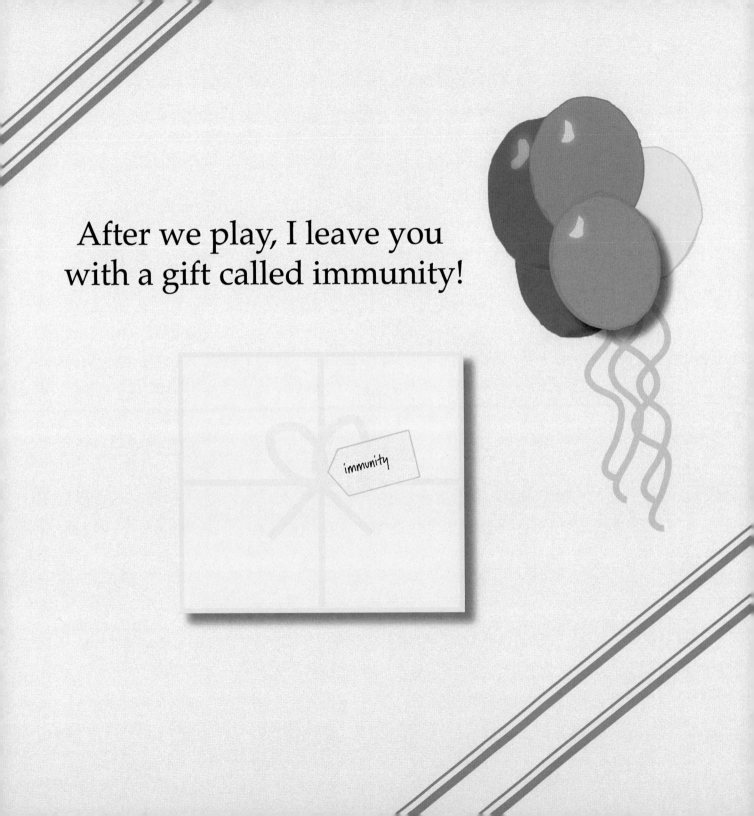

Immunity is special cells your body grows so that next time we meet, your body knows how to keep you from getting as sick so quick.

Immunity 'Cell' Soldiers

Thank you, Luna Rona.

I'm glad I learned how to play with you and be safe

You're welcome, Rue!

Remember, talking to each other is what helps us to not be afraid. The more we learn, the more we know, and the better we grow!

Made in the USA
Middletown, DE
21 August 2021